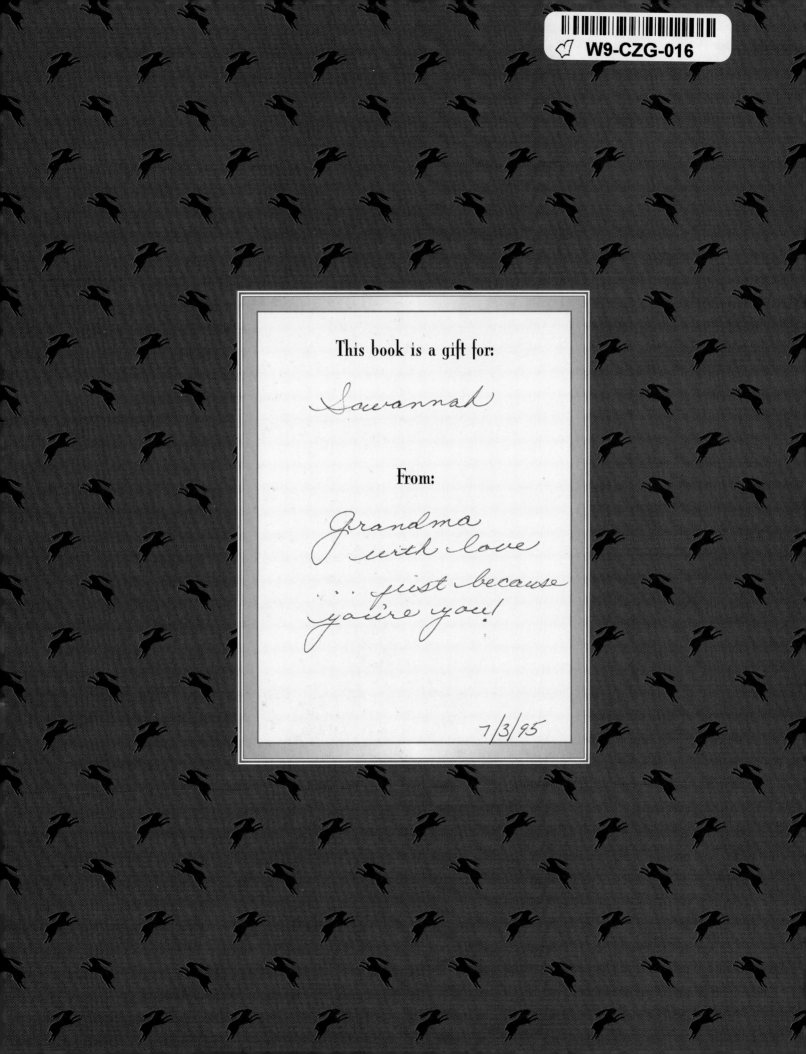

This book is a gift for:

Savannah

From:

Grandma
with love
... just because
you're you!

7/3/95

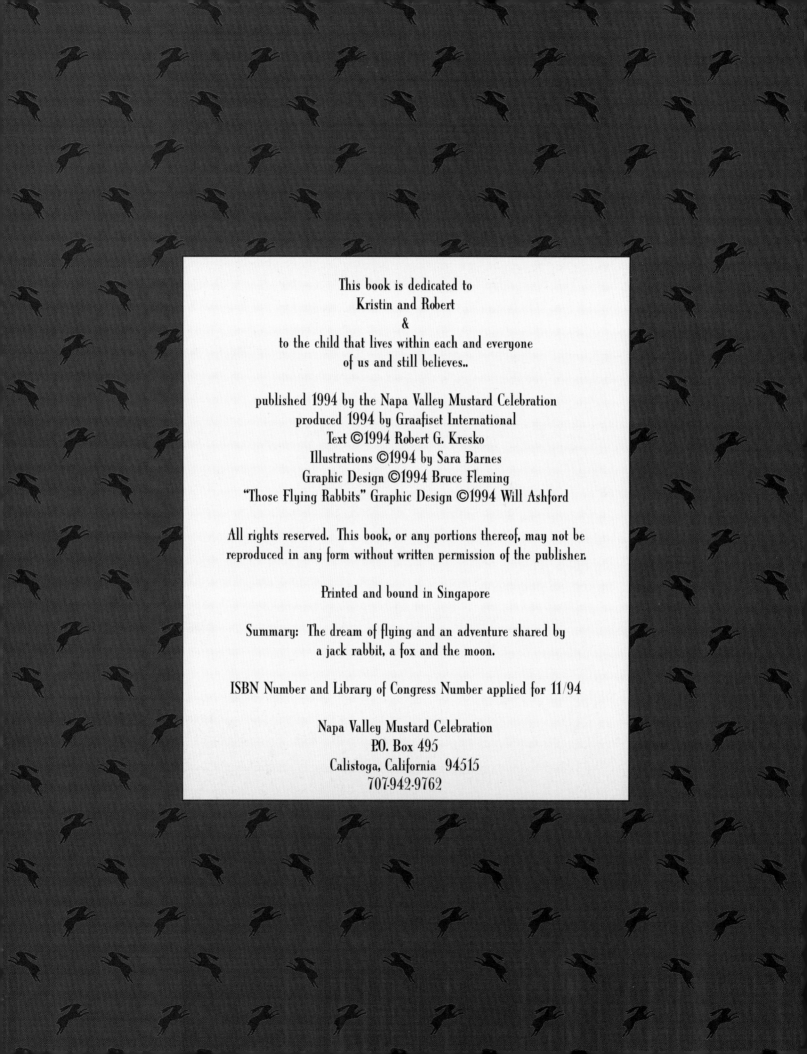

This book is dedicated to
Kristin and Robert
&
to the child that lives within each and everyone
of us and still believes..

published 1994 by the Napa Valley Mustard Celebration
produced 1994 by Graafiset International
Text ©1994 Robert G. Kresko
Illustrations ©1994 by Sara Barnes
Graphic Design ©1994 Bruce Fleming
"Those Flying Rabbits" Graphic Design ©1994 Will Ashford

Printed and bound in Singapore

Summary: The dream of flying and an adventure shared by
a jack rabbit, a fox and the moon.

ISBN Number and Library of Congress Number applied for 11/94

Napa Valley Mustard Celebration
P.O. Box 495
Calistoga, California 94515
707-942-9762

NAPA JACK'S FIRST FLIGHT

Written by Robert G. Kresko   Illustrated by Sara Barnes

There is a little vineyard where the grapes grow red and green

Near a town called Calistoga, or somewhere in between.

And somewhere in that vineyard there's a hole in the ground,

And while it's well hidden, if you look, it can be found.

※

There is a certain furry friend who lives down in that crack.

His last name's Mr. Rabbit, and his first is Napa Jack.

As rabbits go, they're all the same, whether brown or white or black.

They hop and jump and nose around, but not this Napa Jack.

※

You see, he flies, or so they say, and some say that's impossible.

But not for Jack; I'll tell you why... Napa Jack is magical.

He has this special power, and it never gets him flustered.

He knows it happens once a year, in Spring amidst the mustard.

Now, what is this mustard?" you might ask. "Is it something I might eat?"

I'll answer, "Yes, it's a plant which grows in the vineyard at your feet."

Now Napa Jack, he loves these plants... so glad that they abound.

For once a year this mustard helps him fly right off the ground.

&

He was told one time, you must be humble, not boast, not brag nor blab it.

"Not me, you see the reason is that I am Napa Jack Rabbit.

For I can do, what most cannot, and never crow about it.

The mustard plant, it grants my wish.   What would I do without it?"

&

Jack, oh may I call you that, there's something I must know.

How does this plant you love so much help fly you to and fro?

"It happened one night," he detailed, "when the moon was high up in the sky.

I went for a walk, or was it a hop, when someone whispered, 'Napa Jack, don't pass me by.'

I stopped right there wiggled my nose, turned my ears to left and right.

There was nothing unusual I smelled or heard on that starry moonlit night.

So I began to hop, or was it is a jump? My head was in such a muddle.

But again, I heard the voice say to me, 'I'm here; look in this puddle.'

❧

"I looked into the puddle and amazed was I to see

The moon, big and bright, whisp'ring to little ol' me.

'This was quite a sight,' I thought, 'for sure, I must be dreaming.'

'Oh no, you're not; you're wide awake,' said this full moon beaming.

❧

" 'Because you've loved these plants and cared, I'll grant one special thing.

Once a year you'll fly, my friend, if you allow your heart to take wing.

Now here's how you'll do it. Listen close. Here's how you will soar all around.

Just wiggle your nose and waggle your tail and touch your ears... tips to ground.

Say, "Mustard, please, help me fly." Close your eyes. Shut them tight.

Then, my Mr. Napa Jack Rabbit, you'll be soaring through the night.

Believe in yourself, and if you wish real hard to where you want to go.

Have no fear; you'll soon be there; the mustard will make it so.'

☙

Suddenly the wind blew hard, forcing the water to quake and quiver.

This moonlit image danced round and round, making Napa Jack shake and shiver.

The wind stopped at last, the image did fade, disappeared, not to be seen.

It left Jack to wonder, "Did I really see this?" I think you know what I mean.

☙

"I looked all around; 'twas not to be found, oh my... what do I do now?

I shrugged my shoulders, scratched my head, all I could say was, 'Wow!'

I turned around to go back to my home; I ran all the way, or did I hop?

Through mustard grass in moonlit dark, nothing could make me stop.

Well, that's what I thought! At least up till now, for something was blocking my way.

It was big, dark and furry, so I wanted to hurry, to get home without delay.

I stopped in my tracks, or did I slow down? Oh well, as if it mattered.

It was a fox in front of me; he was wearing a hat; it was quite tattered.

✦

"There's something else I should mention, for he was such an amazing sight.

He had a goatee and was wearing sun glasses in the vineyard on that night.

'Oh why, Mr. Fox, do you stand in my way?' I tried to say, when he uttered,

'Hey Napa Jack Rabbit, you'll have to stop here, just you and me in this mustard... you know. '

✦

"I couldn't believe my eyes or his voice... or the hat and shades he wore.

I wanted to run to get out of that place, when he started to speak once more.

'Hey, man... my name is Felix the Fox,' he said with a great big grin on his face.

'You'll have to listen; there's no other way for you to leave this place...my little man. '

my, oh my, what do I do now?" Jack's nose twitched; his tail went on shaking.

'I guess I'll just stay here and listen to him; he's blocking the path I am taking."

"Oh what, oh what, do you want, Felix Fox?' I said in my best rabbit voice.

'Listen, man, I don't do this often,' he snorted, 'but I think I'll give you a choice... dude.'

" 'I'll tell you a riddle which you'll have to guess if you really want to be free.

If you have no answer, then you'll understand, sir, you'll be coming home for dinner with me... you dig?

Now here's the riddle; lend me an ear, and hear this question for you.

Many have tried, but there's only one answer; now listen and hear your clue.' "

Napa Jack was astounded. His little heart pounded, and he said as strong as he could,

"Go ahead, Felix Fox, I'll answer your riddle." Though he wasn't quite sure he would.

Felix replied, "All of life revolves about it, Napa Jack, and fear abounds without it.

In your dreams you've allowed it. Think back. Those who know will never doubt it."

nswer this riddle, I'll give you some time. See that you don't take too long.

I'm restless and hungry, my friend, and you may regret it if you're wrong... get it? "

Oh my, oh my, what's our Jack to do? This is no time for him to be fickle.

"Well, do something now," he started to think, "to get yourself out of this pickle."

৵

Napa Jack thought of the riddle, remembered his dream, there must be some connection.

"What was it the moon had said?" pondered he. "If I could only recall its direction.

If I could only have faith, if I could only... BELIEVE, now wait, I think I know.

All I have to do is remember, and I'll be able to go.

৵

"I'll fly right over Felix's head.   Won't he be surprised!?

I'll move so fast. He won't catch me. He won't believe his eyes."

Well, Felix now was starting to growl, perhaps to show his displeasure.

Napa Jack was growing stronger now, resolved with every measure.

ack closed his eyes, to try out his plan, and he tried for all he was worth.

He wiggled his tail and waggled his ears and touched his nose to the earth...

"Oh, something is wrong; it didn't work," he thought with great dismay;

"I know, I know, I'll make it right; I'll try another way."

❧

Felix was not amused by this, he surely showed no doubt.

He stepped closer to Jack and grunted, "Hey dude, your time's run out! hah."

Napa Jack Rabbit stared straight ahead. His eyes grew big and round.

He wiggled his nose, waggled his tail and touched his ears... tips to ground.

❧

He exclaimed, "Mustard, please help me to fly!" and he believed with all his might.

Remembering what the moon had said, he closed his eyes, shut them tight.

Before he knew it, he left the ground. He was ten feet in the air!

He opened his eyes to look all around, to see this strange affair.

He started to glide as he looked down at a strange and bewildering sight.

Felix Fox doffed his cap, waved and laughed, "Hey dude, have an excellent flight."

"So Felix created a ruse," Jack thought, "to get me to make a decision."

As Jack rose higher, he looked back to see Felix fading from his vision.

※

Our flying Napa Jack smiled with his heart. He was where he wanted to be.

He couldn't deny, it was wondrous to fly. He had the whole world to see.

Well, Napa Jack Rabbit, you'd better grab it, because it's your time to fly.

You're up in the air, with nary a care; tonight you belong to the sky.

※

Oh, what a joy to be in the air, to be free of Earth's gravity.

To soar like a bird, glide on the wind, to dance through an invisible sea.

On the wings of thought you'll ride, in a night that's filled with laughter.

Direct your flight with imagination and a dream of forever after.

hat a night! What a night! What a night !" he giggled, "The best night that ever was!

There's no other way I know to explain it, except, well, 'just because.' "

So much excitement for one little rabbit, Napa Jack was beginning to tire.

Time to go home; he had enough; this midnight-moonlight mustard flier.

❧

He turned for the vineyard, back to his home, his hole so deep in the ground.

He could fly through the sky once more, when the mustard comes round.

Frogs did ribbit; owls were hooting; crickets joined the stirring applause,

As the earth welcomed back the feel again of Napa Jack Rabbit's four paws.

❧

To his hole he scampered, stopping to look in the sky he just flew.

Jack had to look twice; he wasn't quite sure what had just come into his view.

The moon winked, whispering to him, "Napa Jack Rabbit, Good Night."

Home at last, Jack shut his eyes to dream of next year's flight.

There is a little vineyard where the grapes grow red and green.

Near a town called Calistoga, or somewhere in between.

And somewhere in that vineyard, in a hole so very deep,

Our friend, Napa Jack Rabbit, is smiling in his sleep.

Acknowledgements

Napa Jack's First Flight is a story of dreaming of what could be, believing in yourself, and following through to see your dreams become a reality. It is also a story of the magic that can be created with the talents of dedicated writers, artists, actors and producers. The Napa Valley Mustard Celebration is an annual event created to raise funds for the building of a community center for Calistoga, a small city in the upper Napa Valley. In the inaugural year of the Napa Valley Mustard Celebration over 24,000 people came to share in this dream and to celebrate the beauty of the blooming mustard which blankets the valley in a sea of brilliant yellow.

Scott Cooper is a visionary, a dreamer and a producer. As Executive Producer of the Napa Valley Mustard Celebration, Scott conceptualized creating a children's book about the flying rabbit in Sara Barnes' poster painting "Over the Rainbow". His vision for a children's piece of literature was to create the same magic in verse that Sara had created on canvas. As he casually mentioned his idea to friend Gary Huff, he had no idea that he had planted a seed which would blossom like the prolific mustard plants the Celebration commemorates. Gary suggested Robert Kresko, a mutual friend and Celebration supporter, to write the story. The next day eight verses were scribbled onto a sketch pad and Napa Jack's First Flight became a project that would involve the joint efforts of many talented people. Within three weeks the story in rough form was finished and Sara was commissioned to illustrate the book.

Robert was in love with every word he had originally written for this story, but editorial development was inevitable. The editing team for this book consisted of Sylvia Scott, President of the Calistoga Senior Association and founding member of the Calistoga Community Center Project, Dean Witter III, a part-time Calistoga resident and appointed grammarian expert, Neil Murray, freelance editor and former book store owner, Ann Topham, iambic pentameter consultant., and Susan Parker, Executive Director of the Napa Valley Mustard Celebration.

Graphic design for this book was created by Bruce Fleming, Bruce Fleming & Co. The graphic design for the end papers, "Those Flying Rabbits," was created by Will Ashford. The printing production was coordinated by Albert Yokum of Graafiset International.